A Very Witchy Spelling Bee

George Shannon

Illustrated by Mark Fearing

HARCOURT CHILDREN'S BOOKS
Houghton Mifflin Harcourt
Boston   New York   2013

Harcourt Children's Books is an imprint of Houghton Mifflin Harcourt Publishing Company.

www.hmhbooks.com

The illustrations in this book were done in pencil and then altered digitally.
The text type was set in Grandma.
The display type was set in Dominican and Jester.

Library of Congress Cataloging-in-Publication Data
Shannon, George.
A very witchy spelling bee / George Shannon ; illustrated by Mark Fearing.
pages cm
Summary: Little witch Cordelia loves to spell, but can she beat the long-time champion
in the Witches' Spelling Bee?
ISBN 978-0-15-206696-3
[1. Spelling bees—Fiction. 2. English language—Spelling—Fiction. 3. Witches—Fiction.]
I. Fearing, Mark, illustrator. II. Title.
PZ7.S5287Ve 2013
[E]—dc23
2012045935

Manufactured in China
SCP 10 9 8 7 6 5 4 3 2 1
4500409301

For Cordelia Whitman—G.S.

For Mom, who was never witchy,
even after helping me study for spelling tests—M.F.

Cordelia loved broccoli, spelling, and snakes.
She even liked to spell when she spoke.
"Mama, please pass, P-A-S-S, the broccoli."

She spent so much time studying spelling and practicing spells, her mother had to *make* her go outside to play. Even then, she played by mixing her spelling with spells.

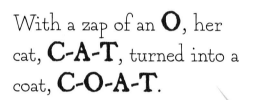

With a zap of an **O**, her cat, **C-A-T**, turned into a coat, **C-O-A-T**.

Then back to a cat.

The zap of a **K** turned the very same cat into a tack, **T-A-C-K**.

No one ever knew what they'd find in her yard.

One day in the park, Cordelia cried, "Look, Mama, look! It's a sign, **S-I-G-N**, meant for me." "You're so young," said her mother. "Perhaps you should wait."

Cordelia shook her head and said,
"No. I've studied. I've practiced.
I'm ready to win!"

News quickly spread. Until now the youngest contestant had been fifty-two. The most recent winner was Beulah Divine, age two hundred and three.

When *she* heard the news, she smirked with delight and a wretched glee. "I've won thirteen times, and I *will* win again. Beating a child will be twice as much fun!"

On the dark, stormy night of the double spelling bee, the stage was filled with the spellers and things to be spelled.

"Remember the rules!" cried a pumpkin-shaped witch.

1. When your name is called, pull a letter out of the bowl.

2. Choose something onstage and spell it.

3. Using the letter you picked, cast a spell that transforms what you chose into something new.

4. Spell the new word.

Opal went first and pulled out an **M**.
With a wave of her wand, she turned
ice, **I-C-E**, into mice, **M-I-C-E**.

Gladys was next, but it didn't go well.
When she pulled out a **Z**, she panicked and ran!

Madge got a **C** and trembled at first,
then handily changed a lock, **L-O-C-K**,
to a clock, **C-L-O-C-K**.

Zelda pulled out an **S**, saw the hoe,
and grinned. She transformed that
hoe, **H-O-E**, into a shoe, **S-H-O-E**.

Cordelia stood with her head held high. She walked to the bowl and pulled out an **R**. Without even a pause, Cordelia turned Zelda's new shoe, **S-H-O-E**, into a horse, **H-O-R-S-E**. The crowd oohed and ahhed.

"I think she could win," said her mother with pride.

Beulah was next. She cackled and hissed. "Now it's time for the fun to begin!"

Her letter was **O**. She zapped Madge's cat, **C-A-T**, into a taco, **T-A-C-O**.

The audience gasped. Madge petted her taco and sobbed, "I quit!"

After that, the witches still left were so nervous,
they all made mistakes. Poor Helen Jeanette's
was the worst one of all. She intended to change
a stuffed owl into a bowl, but her quivering finger aimed
at a pumpkin instead. When a letter-spell zaps an object
and can't make a new word . . . that object explodes!

By the time all the pumpkin remains had been cleared,
there were only two spellers left on the stage:
Cordelia and Beulah Divine.

Cordelia took a deep breath and gritted her teeth.
"I studied. I practiced. I'm ready to win!"

She pulled out an **L**, aimed her spell at a map, **M-A-P**,
and easily had a new lamp, **L-A-M-P**.

Beulah Divine's next letter was **P**, and things only got worse. With a two-fingered spell, she zapped Cordelia's ears, **E-A-R-S**, into . . . pears, **P-E-A-R-S**.

The audience hissed.

Despite her new pears,
Cordelia stood firm.
"I studied. I practiced.
I'm ready to win!"

She pulled out a **W**,
then gracefully changed
a plain ear of corn, **C-O-R-N**,
into a crown, **C-R-O-W-N**.

Beulah snorted and cackled as she picked out a **C**.
"Let me think." She glared at Cordelia, and then in a zap,
Cordelia's hair, **H-A-I-R**, turned into a . . .

chair, **C-H-A-I-R**!
Now the audience shrieked.
"She's vile! She's evil!"

Cordelia's mother jumped up and screamed,
"She's a jealous old *fiend!*"

Beulah sneered at the crowd. "I'm a *what?*"
The barn fell so quiet, nothing was heard but the heartbeats of bats.
"Never mind," snorted Beulah, turning back to the bowl.
"Let's get this thing over. I'm ready to win. And I *don't* want to wait."

Cordelia's next letter was **R**.
She nervously looked at the items
still left on the stage. A sweater.
A hankie. A bowl full of slugs.
Nothing onstage could be changed
with an **R**. Unless—

Beulah cackled again.
"Is our little Cordelia stuck?"

"Not a bit. I studied. I practiced. I'm ready to win!"
Cordelia stared deep into Beulah's small eyes
and zapped out a spell with a two-footed stomp.
Beulah shivered and twitched, snorted and groaned,
as her snarl slowly changed to a large, toothy grin.

"Snookums, my pal!" Beulah said with a squeal.
"I quit. You win!"

Cordelia gasped. Her mother cried, "Yes!"
Every witch, young and old, sat stunned and relieved.
Beulah Divine was no longer a fiend, **F-I-E-N-D**.
With one letter, one spell, Cordelia had turned
Beulah Divine into a friend, **F-R-I-E-N-D**.